TABLE OF CONTENTS

My GOVERNMENT

Standing in the Vice President's Shoes

Kaitlyn Duling

Cavendish Square
New York

The president and vice president both work in the White House.

INTRODUCTION

The White House is not a normal house. Sure, there are bedrooms. There are kitchens. There is a yard. A big one! The president and his family live there. The president and vice president work there. They work together. They talk with other leaders. They sign bills into law. They help keep us safe. They help keep us healthy and happy. They are called the **executive branch**.

The president and vice president work with Congress. Members of Congress write laws. The Supreme Court makes sure the laws are working. All three parts of the government are needed. They are called **branches**. They balance each other. Each job is important.

Sometimes the vice president meets with politicians from other countries.

CHAPTER ONE

The Responsibilities of the Vice President

The official list of duties of the vice president is short. He is the president's helper. If the president dies, or chooses to stop being president, then the vice president takes over. The vice president must be ready. He might need to be the president. This has happened nine times.

The vice president is also the president of the United States Senate. The Senate is part of Congress. They turn bills into laws. The vice president helps in the Senate sometimes. But he does not lead Senate meetings.

The vice president and the president run for office together.

The senators choose someone else to do that. The vice president is not allowed to **debate**. He is not allowed to give speeches. The vice president just listens. In fact, he usually does not vote. The vice president only votes if there is a tie. The vice president's other title, president of the Senate, is large. However, his role there is small.

At **election** time, the vice president has a fun job. Elections for president occur every four years. The big vote happens in November. The votes are counted quickly. Usually we know the winner on the same day, or very soon after. Then, we wait many weeks. The vice president gets the official **ballots** on January 6. The vice president opens them. They are counted. This happens in front of Congress. It is a big day!

Sometimes vice presidents run for president. They still open the ballots. It can be tense. They might say their

The vice president gives speeches and tries to help people.

Joe Biden, a former vice president, opens the ballots and reads them.

own name. Winner! Or they might read their rival's name. Only four vice presidents have read their own names.

Being vice president can prepare someone to be president. In fact, the vice president helps the president each day. Some say the vice president has many "chores." He goes to meetings with the **cabinet**. The cabinet is full of different experts. They meet together and give advice to the president. One cabinet member is a farming expert.

One knows about jobs. There are twenty-four members of the cabinet, including the vice president.

The vice president helps in other ways. He has special groups to lead. He gives speeches. The vice president meets with people from other countries. Vice presidents serve on the **National Security Council**. This group is part of the executive branch. The National Security Council helps the president with security. The Central Intelligence Agency (CIA) is often involved with National Security Council meetings. The vice president stays busy!

Who the Vice President Serves

The vice president serves all Americans. He might be the president someday! He has many roles around Washington, DC. The Senate counts on him. The National Security Council needs him. The cabinet needs him, too.

The vice president works hard every single day.

CHAPTER TWO

A Day in the Life of the Vice President

The vice president's job is not silly. He makes decisions. The vice president is a helper. Each day at work is different. He has many duties. The vice president's calendar looks a little crazy. The vice president must be ready for anything.

MORNING

Each morning, the vice president begins the day. He travels about 3 miles (4.8 kilometers) to the White House. He has his own office. Well, it is not too private. The vice president's office is only 50 feet (15 meters) from the **Oval Office**. The Oval Office is where the president works!

The vice president's mansion is beautiful!

They work together often. It helps that they are close together. They can talk. They can have meetings.

The president and vice president meet each week. They think and plan. The vice president has his own aides. These are official helpers. They assist him with all kinds of things.

The Vice President's Home

We all remember the president's famous house. Did you know the vice president has his own official home, too? The vice president lives in a big mansion. It has thirty-three rooms and a pool!

The Vice President's Desk

The vice president has a special desk in his office. It was first used by Teddy Roosevelt in 1902. Since the 1940s, nearly every vice president has signed the desk. The signatures are on the inside of one of the drawers.

AFTERNOON

Sometimes the vice president has lunch with the president. They talk about specific issues. The vice president has more meetings after lunch. He works on special tasks. He talks on the phone. There is so much to do! In the past, vice presidents did not travel or give speeches. Today, the vice president does both.

Often, the vice president helps the president talk to the public. In the afternoon, he might do an interview. He talks on the radio or on television. He talks about ideas and goals. He reports on what is happening in the White House. He supports the president.

Vice presidents enjoy hosting parties in the mansion.

EVENING

The vice president hosts dinners and parties. These events happen at night. They happen on the weekend. He uses his house for events. Members of the **media** are often invited. These are people who report the news. Writers are part of the media. People who take pictures and videos are, too. They take fun pictures at the parties.

Vice President Joe Biden's favorite event was an annual picnic. At the party, he would play with super soakers! Kids and adults all ran around with water guns. Vice President Al Gore had Halloween parties. He liked to dress as a mummy. Being the vice president is work *and* play!

CONCLUSION

Each day is different for the vice president. He works on projects. He supports the president. And he has fun! Many vice presidents have children at home. Their spouses have jobs outside the White House. They exercise. They eat dinner. They are just like you and me. Well, almost.

The Vice President's Jet

The president travels in a private jet. It is called Air Force One. What about the vice president? He rides in Air Force Two. This plane will take him anywhere in the world!

Barack Obama and Joe Biden were running mates and friends.

CHAPTER THREE

Becoming the Vice President

Do you want to run for vice president? There are rules. You must have been born in the United States. You must be at least thirty-five years old. You also must have lived in the United States for fourteen years. Those are the only three rules. Many vice presidents were members of Congress first. Some were governors. Some also served in the military. All have had at least some government experience before becoming vice president.

Election Day happens every four years in November. That's when we choose the president. It's when we choose the vice president, too. They run as a set. They are called

John McCain and Sarah Palin each attracted different kinds of voters.

running mates. Usually running mates are different from each other. They balance each other. Together they represent a political party.

There are two main political parties: Democrat and Republican. The two groups have long histories. They have very different beliefs. These parties choose their own **candidates**. Candidates are people who try to get a job. Before an election, the party members meet. It is a big meeting. They vote to decide on candidates. They have to convincc pcople to vote for their candidates. One of the parties will win. One will lose. Everyone hopes they chose strong candidates.

The candidate for vice president might have a famous name. This candidate might be from a different part of the United States. The candidate might have a special past. Hopefully this helps with the votes. Sometimes this works. Sometimes it doesn't.

Vice presidential candidates have their own debates.

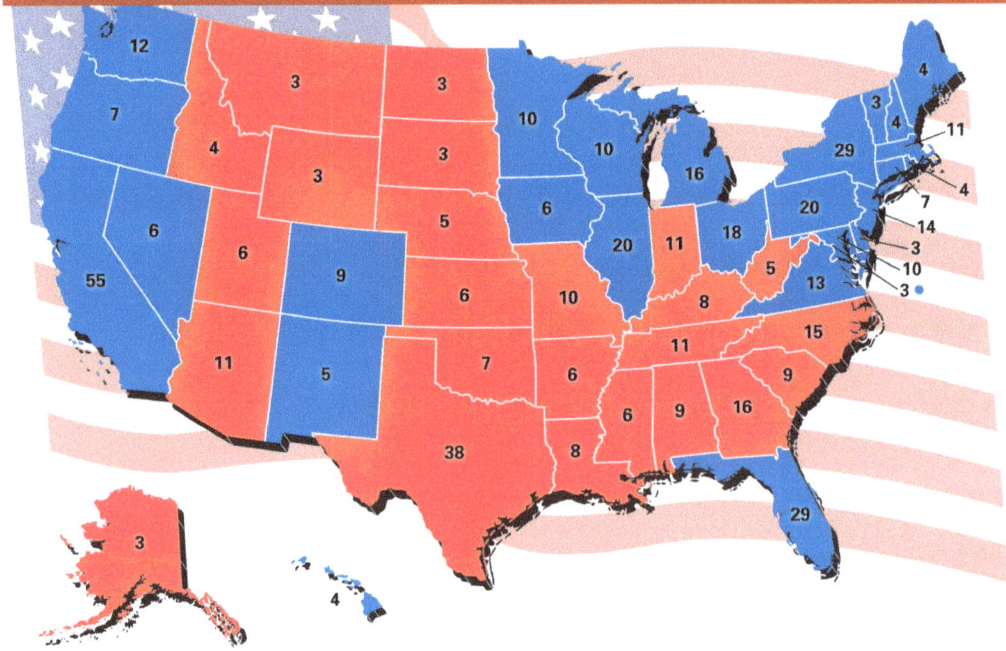

This map shows the number of electoral votes each state had in the 2012 presidential election. The blue states voted for Barack Obama and the red states voted for Mitt Romney.

On Election Day in November, we all think we vote for the vice president and president. But we actually vote for people called **electors**. The ballot might say the candidates' names. But the people are voting for electors. In December, the electors meet and vote. This meeting is called the **Electoral College**. Electors promise to support a candidate. The electors vote for vice president and president separately. It can be a little confusing!

Each state has a number of electors. That number is based on the number of people in the state. Some states have many electoral votes. California is big. It has many votes. Some states only have a few.

The president takes an oath of office. The vice president takes one too. They both make a promise to serve the country. The vice president's job lasts at least four years. It could last eight years. But the president can only serve two terms. Vice presidents can serve as many terms as they win. Only two vice presidents served with more than one president. They must have loved their jobs!

A Female Vice President?

Why have we not had a female vice president? There have only been two female candidates. The Democratic Party nominated Geraldine Ferraro in 1984. The Republicans nominated Sarah Palin in 2008. Hopefully more women will run and win!

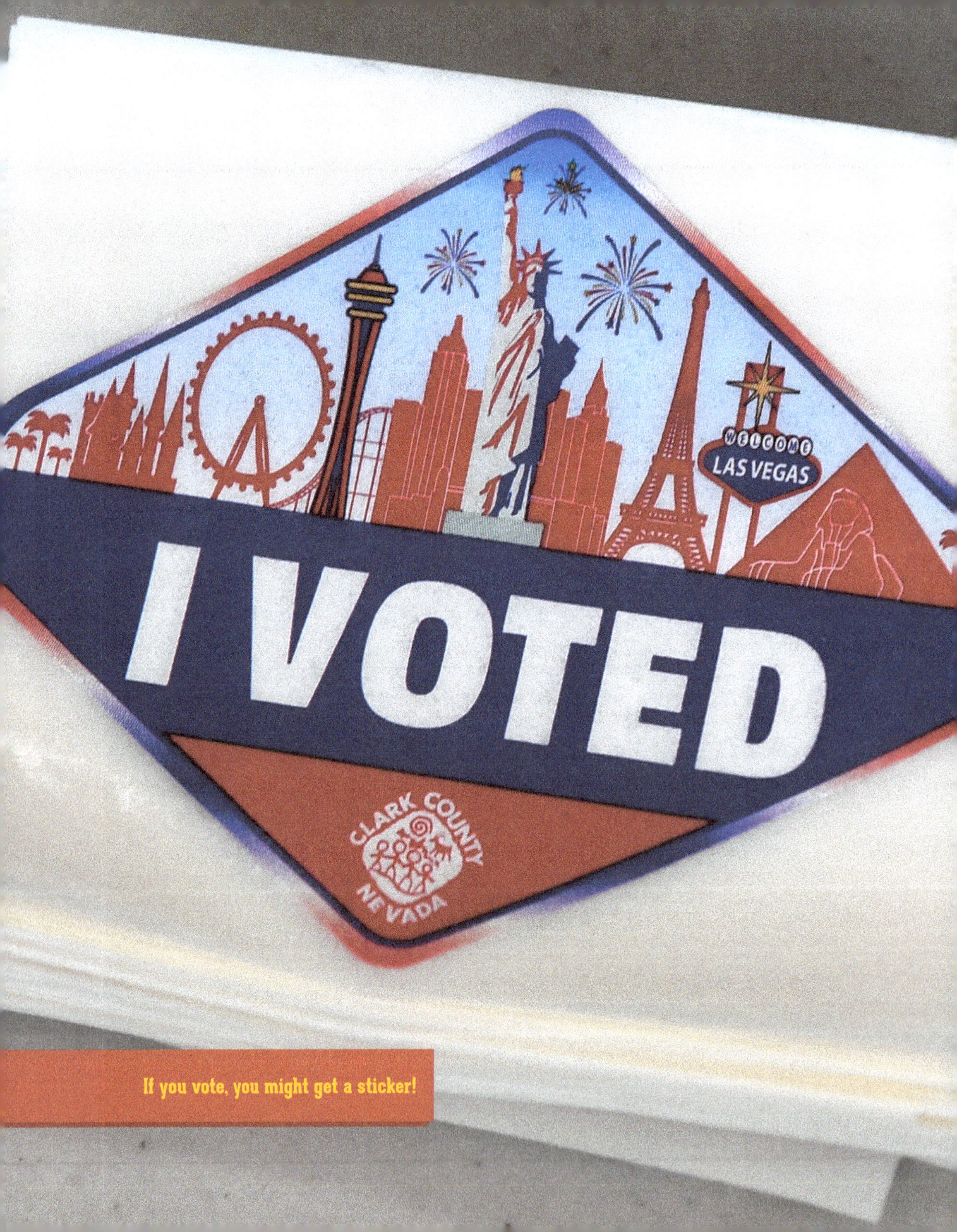

If you vote, you might get a sticker!

CHAPTER FOUR

How Can You Get Involved?

So, are you thinking about running for office? The vice president's job does sound like fun! Vice presidents do all kinds of things. They are helpers. Do you like to help? This job might be for you. Women can run for office. Men can run for office. Even kids can get involved!

The job has many meetings. It has many roles. You would support the president. You would be on the radio and on television. You would be careful about what you say and do. Each day is different. You could do it!

The vice president meets with many different people.

To work in the executive branch, get started now. To go far, you need good grades. Listen in class. Do your homework. Someday, you could go to college. In college, you will learn more about the government. You will learn about people. You will learn about big issues. You will learn how to help those around you. You can start doing that today!

Listen and think about the lives of others. Ask your parents about the news. Read the newspaper. The more you read, the more you will know. This will make it easier to help people. Helping people is a huge part of a politician's job.

On Election Day in November, your parents will vote. Ask if you can go with them! You can watch them vote. It might be on a computer. It might be on a piece of paper. You can see who is running for vice president.

You might want to learn more about the government. You can read about it online. You can watch politicians on television. You will probably have feelings and opinions about what they say. Tell them! Write them letters. Call

Votes are kept private with voting booths or dividers.

Reading is a great way to learn more about the government!

them on the phone. Send them emails. You can find their contact information on the computer. Tell them what is important to you. Do you care about jobs? Schools? Health care? Let them know!

Someday, if you work hard, you can be the vice president. You can meet with the president. You can help the president make decisions. You can be in line for the presidency. What a cool job! We need people with energy for this job. We need people who are honest. We need people who work hard and listen well. Is this you? It could be!

Get Involved!

Elections can be fun! Find out where people near you go to vote. You can go there during an election. Talk to the workers. Ask them questions. Maybe they will let you volunteer. That could be a great way to learn!

GLOSSARY

ballots Pieces of paper or screens on which people mark their votes in an election.

branch One of three parts of the federal government.

cabinet A formal group of advisors to the president.

candidate A person who is trying to get a job or obtain a position.

debate To discuss a topic in a formal meeting.

election The process of choosing by vote.

Electoral College A group of people, representing the states, who vote for the election of president and vice president.

electors People who promise to support a certain candidate and vote in the Electoral College.

executive branch The branch of the federal government that is responsible for supporting and enforcing the laws.

GLOSSARY

media The main forms of communicating information.

National Security Council The committee that advises the president on security matters.

Oval Office The President's formal office in the White House.

running mates Two people who run together for president and vice president.

FIND OUT MORE!

BOOKS

Burns, Ken. *Grover Cleveland, Again!: A Treasury of American Presidents.* New York: Knopf Books for Young Readers, 2016.

DiPucchio, Kelly. *Grace for President.* New York: Disney-Hyperion, 2012.

Landau, Elaine. *The President, Vice President, and Cabinet: A Look at the Executive Branch*. Minneapolis: Lerner Publishing Group, 2012.

WEBSITES

Ben's Guide to the Executive Branch
https://bensguide.gpo.gov/a-executive

iCivics
https://www.icivics.org

Kids.gov
https://kids.usa.gov

MEET THE AUTHOR

Kaitlyn Duling believes in the power of words to change hearts, minds, and, ultimately, actions. A poet, nonfiction author, and grant writer who grew up in Illinois, she now resides in Pittsburgh, Pennsylvania, where she works aboard a bookmobile and helps kids learn to love to read. She knows that knowledge of the past is the key to our future and wants to make sure that all children and families have access to high-quality information. She loves to visit Washington, DC, and see the monuments.

INDEX